MW00743601

DRUG DANGERS

INHALANT DRUG DANGERS

Judy Monroe

St. Elizabeth Ann Seton Middle School
1601 Three Mile Road North
Traverse City, MI 49686

Enslow Publishers, Inc.

40 Industrial Road   PO Box 38
Box 398   Aldershot
Berkeley Heights, NJ 07922 Hants GU12 6BP
USA   UK

http://www.enslow.com

Library of Congress Cataloging-in-Publication Data

Monroe, Judy
    Inhalant drug dangers / Judy Monroe.
        p. cm. — (Drug dangers)
    Includes bibliographical references and index.
    Summary: Describes the dangers of inhaling all kinds of chemical
products, including paints, gasoline, aerosols, glues, and more, and
discusses the signs of inhalant abuse and where to go for help.
    ISBN 0-7660-1153-4
      1. Solvent abuse—United States—Juvenile literature. 2. Teenagers—
Substance use—United States—Juvenile literature. [1. Solvent abuse.
2. Substance abuse.] I. Title. II. Series.
HV5825.M63   1999   98-33668
362.29'9—dc21   CIP
                                                 AC

Printed in the United States of America

10 9 8 7 6 5 4 3

To Our Readers:
All Internet Addresses in this book were active and appropriate when we
went to press. Any comments or suggestions can be sent by e-mail to
Comments@enslow.com or to the address on the back cover.

Photo Credits: Corel Corporation, pp. 7, 10, 13, 15, 19, 21, 31, 33, 36,
44, 52; Díamar Interactive Corp., pp. 23, 47, 54; U.S. National Library of
Medicine, p. 26 (both).

Cover Photo: Enslow Publishers, Inc.

contents

Titles in the **Drug Dangers** series:

Alcohol Drug Dangers
0-7660-1735-4 Paperback
0-7660-1159-3 Library ed.

Crack and Cocaine Drug Dangers
0-7660-1736-2 Paperback
0-7660-1155-0 Library ed.

Diet Pill Drug Dangers
0-7660-1737-0 Paperback
0-7660-1158-5 Library ed.

Heroin Drug Dangers
0-7660-1738-9 Paperback
0-7660-1156-9 Library ed.

Inhalant Drug Dangers
0-7660-1739-7 Paperback
0-7660-1153-4 Library ed.

Marijuana Drug Dangers
0-7660-1740-0 Paperback
0-7660-1214-X Library ed.

Speed and Methamphetamine Drug Dangers
0-7660-1741-9 Paperback
0-7660-1157-7 Library ed.

Steroid Drug Dangers
0-7660-1742-7 Paperback
0-7660-1154-2 Library ed.

one

Ian's Story

When Ian was twelve, his life changed a lot. First his parents divorced. Then Ian, his younger brother, and his mother moved from Minnesota to Oklahoma. That is when he started drinking alcohol and smoking pot (marijuana).

Two years later, Ian moved back to Minnesota to live with his father. One day, Ian's best friend showed him how to use inhalants, chemicals that give off fumes and are inhaled for the "high" they produce. "I remember sitting in my room with a can of fabric protector. My friend told me it was a good high. I remember getting an intense high. And then I inhaled again."[1]

His friend told him which inhalants to use and how to do it. Ian's favorites—fabric protector and leather protector—were what he inhaled on and off for a year. Ian usually inhaled these chemicals alone, in secret. Sometimes, though, a friend who also used inhalants joined him.

Ian never told his father, his girlfriend, or other friends about his inhalant use. "I was afraid my friends wouldn't like me if they knew I was inhaling, so I didn't do it around them or tell them about it," he said.[2]

His chemical use began to interfere with his everyday life. He remembered, "I ditched school so many times the school finally kicked me out. So my dad told me he was sending me back to my mom's house."[3]

A Broken Promise

Returning to Oklahoma at fifteen, Ian continued to buy and inhale from cans of leather protector. A new friend, also an inhalant user, introduced him to other kinds of inhalants. Two years later Ian left his mother's home. He moved into an apartment with a friend. For a few months, he drank alcohol, smoked marijuana, and continued to inhale chemicals.

Ian soon found that it cost a lot to pay rent and buy drugs. So he moved back in with his mother. Soon she caught him inhaling gasoline. She told him inhaling gas could kill him, then ordered him to move out. After a long bus ride back to Minnesota, Ian again moved in with his father. This time, his dad insisted on no drug use— including inhalants. Ian agreed.

But he did not keep his promise. Just five months later, Ian's dad caught him inhaling leather protector. He put Ian, eighteen, into a drug treatment program. After three months of hard work in full-time treatment, Ian graduated to a daytime job-training program. In the evenings, he went to treatment.

Common household products in spray cans, everything from fabric protector to underarm deodorant, provide an all-too-easy means for inhaling.

What Ian Learned Too Late

Unfortunately, Ian learned about the problems that inhalants cause only after he stopped using them. "If I knew what inhalants [could] do, I would never have started," he said.[4]

"I'm worried now that I might have continued brain damage. I get a lot of headaches. And sometimes things happen—like the other day I was at work counting chicken pieces in boxes. All I had to do was [quickly look inside] each box to see if a certain number was in there. I couldn't do it. I've always been really good at math, but I couldn't do a quick count of the chicken pieces in the box. It's hard for me to concentrate—my mind wanders and I find myself daydreaming."[5]

His drug and inhalant use has also caused problems between Ian and his noninhaling friends and his parents. He said, "I lost my dad's trust when he caught me inhaling the last time I lived with him."[6]

His drug use may harm yet another person. Ian's girlfriend is pregnant. "I'm concerned," he admitted about the effects of his inhalant use on his unborn baby.[7]

two

The Silent Epidemic

The National Inhalant Prevention Coalition (NIPC) calls inhalant use a "silent epidemic."[1] This organization in Austin, Texas, says that inhalant use is a fast-growing problem across the United States. The NIPC tracks national drug use. Recently, it reported that inhalant use has increased every year since the late 1980s.[2] Why is this happening? Health experts point to the following reasons:

- Many common, cheap household and school products can be inhaled.

- Inhalant products are legal and easy to find at home or school. Anyone can buy them at neighborhood stores.

- Inhalant use is often hard to detect. People can easily miss signs of teen inhalant use.

- Inhalants act quickly on the mind and body.

♦ Many people do not know about the dangers of inhalants. This includes teens, teachers, parents, and other adults.

Sound the Alarm

For many reasons, we all need to be concerned about this epidemic. First, even if used only once, inhalants can kill. Many teens are not aware of this risk. In Englewood, Colorado, paramedics had to work fast to save the life of an eleven-year-old girl. She almost died from sniffing hair spray. A paramedic explained, "What happens is the person gets hallucinations [imaginary sights, sounds, or

Used even once, inhalants, such as hair spray, can kill. Teens are at an especially high risk of harm from inhalants, because their bodies are still growing and developing.

feelings] and an intense sense of euphoria [high] that lasts for a short time. You can do it once and it can kill you."[3]

Also, compared with adults, teens are at higher risk of inhalant harm. Inhalants can damage the minds and bodies of teens because their bodies are still growing and developing. The International Institute of Inhalant Abuse (IIIA) in Englewood, Colorado, explained that inhalants are more dangerous than any other drug. "Inhalants are industrial chemicals. They are not meant to be consumed or put into the body. Yet kids are putting them into their bodies in very high amounts."[4]

Another problem is that inhalants are often the first substance teens try. Inhalant use sometimes lures teens to try other drugs such as alcohol, tobacco, or marijuana. That is why inhalants are called gateway drugs. A gateway drug leads to other illegal drug use. Ian, the teen from the first chapter, agrees. "I haven't met anyone who uses only inhalants."[5]

Researchers find that younger teens use inhalants more than older teens do. In fact, until the eighth grade, inhalants rank as the third most commonly used drug. Only alcohol and tobacco rate higher. Then, in the ninth and tenth grades, marijuana use tops inhalant use. Inhalants drop to number four, after alcohol, tobacco, and marijuana. However, inhalants are becoming more popular with college students and older adults.

Female teens are using at about the same rate as male teens. Teens from rich, middle-class, and poor families alike use inhalants. So do young people of various races, whether they live in cities, towns, or rural communities. Inhalant abuse is *not* limited to any one group of people.

Outside the United States, inhalant abuse is also a problem in Africa, Asia, and Latin America.

Who's Using?

Teens are the main users of inhalants. Here are some grim statistics about teen use.

The Numbers: American Teens Who Use Inhalants

- One out of ten teens reports past or current inhalant use.[6]
- More than one million teens, ages twelve to seventeen, tried inhalants in the past year.[7]
- Ian, the teen from the first chapter, is one of 12 million people, ages twelve and older, who have inhaled chemicals at least one time.[8]
- Current use is highest among eighth graders.[9]
- Researchers at the National Institute on Drug Abuse (NIDA) report that almost 22 percent—one out of five—of America's eighth graders have tried inhalants.[10]
- First-time users of inhalants are between seven and seventeen years old.[11] The average age of first-time use is under thirteen.[12] Researchers report that children as young as four or five have used inhalants.

Why Teens Use Inhalants

Ian explained why he used inhalants. "They were cheap, available, and easy to find."[13] Inhalants cost less than alcohol and marijuana, and he could buy them in many stores or look for them at home. He could choose from a wide variety of inhalants.

Many teens abuse inhalants because they believe nothing bad will happen to them. Other teens say they inhale because they are bored, want to get high fast, or want to be cool and do the "in" thing. One teen reported, "It [cans or bottles] can be easily concealed in my pocket and nobody knows."[14] Still others do not know the dangerous facts about inhalants. However, even when armed with information about the harmful effects of inhalants, some teens still use them.

Matt tried inhalants when he was twelve.

> I would do Liquid Paper™ in class. I would put a little on notebook paper and would sniff it. I liked the attention from kids who asked me what I was doing. I knew it killed brain cells big time, but my attitude was I really didn't care. I just liked the feeling.[15]

He began to sniff gasoline, paint thinner, lacquer, and

Many teens, even those who are made aware of inhalants' harmful effects, use them believing that nothing bad will happen to them. Automobile gasoline, a readily available item, is often inhaled.

other inhalants. The first time Matt inhaled gasoline, he felt he could not breathe. He got scared, but he kept sniffing inhalants. He also knew these chemicals were hurting him. He remembered losing his balance and getting bad headaches. "I kept doing more and more. I don't know why," he said.[16] More than three years later, he entered a drug treatment program.

Sometimes teens who abuse inhalants turn friends or family members on to inhaling. While in Oklahoma, Ian taught his younger brother how to inhale chemicals. But some of these teens, after seeing the harmful effects of inhalant use, never start.

Other Names

Use of inhalants goes by a variety of names: sniffing, huffing, bagging, snorting, hacking, glading, and spraying are some of the terms it is known by. All of these names describe the way people inhale chemicals. Directly ingesting and spraying inhalants are especially toxic (poisonous) methods.

Said one emergency medical technician in Kansas City, Kansas:

> We got a 911 call about a kid in a coma. It seems three of them were inhaling a waterproofing spray and this one kid did too much. Basically, he starved his head of oxygen because the spray temporarily replaced the oxygen. It took him three months to recover.[17]

Bagging means placing the inhalant in a plastic or paper bag and inhaling. This method limits the amount of oxygen users get and concentrates the amount of chemicals inhaled.

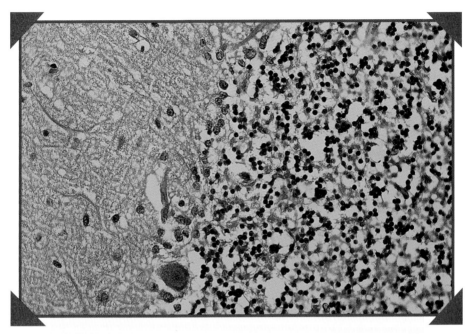

Normal brain tissue is shown. Inhalants can starve the brain of oxygen—an essential ingredient for normal function. Once brain tissue is altered, the effects are irreversible.

The Law

The federal government does not regulate, or control, inhalant sales or misuse. Many states, though, have created their own laws. As of 1997, thirty-six states had inhalant laws. These laws prevent the sale and distribution of various inhalants to teens and children. Other states are working to pass or expand their inhalant laws.[18]

Law enforcement officers, health workers, and teachers are often not trained to recognize the signs of inhalant abuse. Many do not know that inhalant abuse is a serious problem among teens and preteens.

Looking for Signs

To a person who does not know what to look for, inhalant abuse is sometimes hard to spot.

Sometimes people are alerted to inhalant abuse because particular items appear on or near the user. These items are sometimes found in the user's trash, bedroom, or school locker.

The Signs Everyone Missed

Brad, fourteen, was soon to start high school in Broken Arrow, Oklahoma, a suburb of Tulsa. One afternoon, he was relaxing on a friend's back porch, to keep out of the hot August sun. Another friend, Brandon, wandered over

Warning Signs of Inhalant Use

The person who is inhaling generally has two or more of the following persistent problems:

- Chest pain
- Constant cough
- Headaches
- Nausea or upset stomach
- Poor memory and inability to concentrate
- Red or runny nose
- Seizures
- Sores or rashes around the mouth and nose or at the back of the throat
- Stomach pain
- Tremors or shaking hands

Other Signs That May Indicate Inhalant Use

- Acting or looking drunk, but without the smell of alcohol
- Appetite loss, sudden weight loss
- Chemical smell on breath, skin, clothes, or in the bedroom
- Dazed or dizzy look
- Less interest or concern about clothing, grooming, friends, hobbies, sports
- Red, irritated eyes
- Slurred speech
- Soda cans, rags, or sandwich bags with a chemical smell
- Stains on clothing and skin
- Unusual mood changes: being aggressive, irritable, angry, or having "I don't care" attitude

with a can of Scotchgard™. Holding it out, Brandon said, "I heard at school that you can inhale this stuff."[19]

Brad nodded. He'd heard the same thing. Curious, both teens decided to huff the stain repellent. Brandon did not like the high or the bad smell. He vowed not to huff again.

Brad, though, liked how the inhalant made him feel. By the time school started that fall, he was huffing a few times a week. By October, Brad's friends noticed that he was huffing every day and trying different types of inhalants. Brandon told Brad to quit. Brad agreed and threw away the can of butane lighter fluid he was about to inhale.[20]

Not long after that, Brad again was caught with

Things People Use to Abuse Inhalants

- Aerosol spray cans
- Balloons
- Butane lighters
- Canisters
- Cans, bottles, or other containers of inhalants
- Plastic bags
- Socks or rags
- Soda cans

inhalants. This time, the mother of Brad's friend Kelly confronted Brad. Kelly's mother was a nurse. She explained that Brad could seriously damage his lungs. Once more, Brad promised to stop using. He again did not keep his promise.

By January, Brad began failing tests in school. His mother helped him study, but Brad couldn't pull up his grades. He told his mom, "I don't know what's wrong with me. I just can't remember anything anymore."[21] Early that spring Brad tried out for the school's soccer team. Run-down and with a constant cough, Brad could no longer play. He soon quit the team—but not his inhalant use. Brandon again caught Brad inhaling on April 10. At that time, Brad told his friend that he had passed out several times while huffing Scotchgard™.

That next afternoon, Brad and two other neighborhood teens bought three cans of butane. The three guys drove around for two hours, huffing the entire time. When the teens got out of the car and started walking, Brad fell down. He was still holding his can. Someone called 911. Within minutes, an ambulance arrived and whisked Brad to a hospital emergency room. The emergency team could not revive him.

When Brad's parents arrived at the hospital, they were told that Brad had been huffing butane. "Huffing?" asked his mom. "What's that?"[22]

Early the next morning, Brad died, at fifteen years old, from inhalant overdose. His heart, lungs, and kidneys had stopped working.

After Brad's funeral, his parents began to clean out his room. They found five empty cans of butane. Looking at a collage of his favorite things, they found that Brad had taped a Scotchgard™ label at the top. Clues of Brad's inhalant abuse—empty cans, sliding grades, memory loss, constant coughing, poor health, and moody behavior—were in plain sight, but had been overlooked.

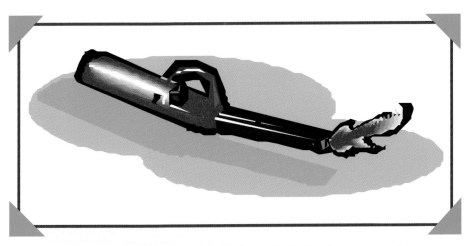

Brad was a casualty of butane lighter fluid, the type used in lighters like this one.

three

Real-Life Stories

The following stories are about teens who used inhalants. Some tried inhalants just once. Others used them regularly. No one, though, could predict what would happen to each teen.

What Inhalants Can Do

Liz, age fifteen, got scared when her hair started falling out. But the Pueblo, Colorado, teen could not stop sniffing paint from milk jugs. She liked the high. But she didn't like how she looked as she lost her appetite and a lot of weight from inhaling the poisonous fumes.[1]

At age eighteen, Billie (not his real name), was in jail for abusing inhalants. For two years, he had huffed paint. Whenever his mom discovered him huffing, she would call the police. Billie has been locked up six times so far.

Said Billie:

I don' t recommend it to them [other young people]. . . it's their brain. It's just a cheap high. The first time I tried it, I got paint all over the front of my clothes because the bag had a hole and I didn't notice until I was walking home. I threw those clothes away.

It seems like I got caught every time I did it. Me and my brother were talking. We decided that paint's nothing but trouble.[2]

Since the early 1990s, rave clubs—dance and party clubs—have popped up across the United States. Rave clubs are a big hit with some teens and young adults. Drug use is common at these places. Poppers (amyl or butyl nitrite capsules that "pop" when broken open for sniffing) often rate as the most popular inhalants.

A seventeen-year-old raver reported, "My roommate uses 'poppers' at 'raves' because he feels it helps his dancing and makes him more lively. It works for him

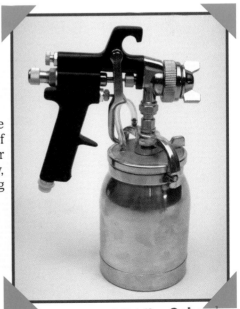

Paint sprayers like this one are used to make the job of painting a large surface easier and faster. Unfortunately, they can also make inhaling easy—and deadly.

some of the time but a couple of times he got dizzy and fell over. The last time he fell over and broke his nose."[3]

Helium balloons filled the party room. A thirteen-year-old teen inhaled helium from a nearby tank. Suddenly, he fell down, unconscious. Then, he had a ten-minute seizure.[4]

The Worst Inhalants Can Do

Each year in the United States, about twelve hundred inhalant-related deaths are reported. However, we do not know the true number of deaths and accidents due to inhalant use. That is because the police or medical examiners may not realize that a death was caused by inhalant use. Instead, they may think that someone died from suicide, suffocation, or an accident.[5]

Here are some teens who paid too high a price for their inhalant use.

- A sixteen-year-old star of her soccer team in North Attleboro, Massachusetts, inhaled butane. The butane was in a can used to refill lighters. Suddenly, her mouth began to foam. She fell down, unconscious. Before anyone could help, her heart stopped, forever.[6]

- In Chester, New Jersey, on December 21, 1993, Justin and his friends filled plastic bags with laughing gas (nitrous oxide). They then put the bags over their mouths and noses or over their heads and inhaled deeply. Justin, age sixteen, collapsed and died.[7]

- On a January night in 1995 in Tipp City, Ohio, Mrs. Miller knocked on the bathroom door. Eric, her athletic twelve-year-old, had been in the bathroom a long time. She called his name several times but heard nothing. Mrs. Miller rattled the doorknob but found it locked. After yelling and knocking for a few minutes, her husband broke down the door.

Eric was in the filled bathtub. Although his head was under water, he had not died from drowning. A deputy from the county sheriff's office found a spray can of airbrush propellant in the bathroom sink. The Millers later found out that Eric had learned how to huff from his classmates. The kids called the inhalants their happy cans.[8]

♦ While in her bedroom, an Arlington, Texas, teen opened a bottle of nail polish dryer and began to sniff the fumes. The thirteen-year-old soon died. Nail polish dryer contains toluene, a poisonous gas.[9]

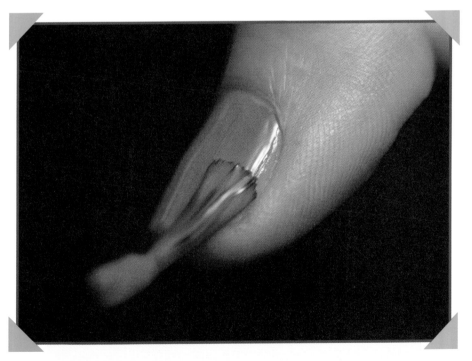

Appearance is very important to most teens. As such, parents would not find it odd to see nail polish dryer around their teen's room. Unfortunately, the chemicals used in it can be toxic if inhaled.

- In February 1994, St. Joseph, Missouri, teens John, Troy, and Tucker were driving around, looking for fun. That evening they were also bagging (sniffing) silver paint fumes in plastic bags. The three decided to call two teen girls on their car phone. One of the girls heard nineteen-year-old Troy say, "OK, boys, we're going to get a good run on it. So whoever wants to get out, better get out now."

  John, the seventeen-year-old driver, turned a corner, gaining speed. The girls heard someone say, "Here we go. We're not stopping. We're not stopping."

  The girls, each on a separate telephone line, heard a crash. Silence filled the telephone wires. Shocked, they called the police.

  The police pulled three teens out of the crumpled car. John and Troy were dead. The other passenger, Tucker, age sixteen, was critically injured. After investigating, the police reported that John had crashed into Mount Mora Cemetery's twelve-foot cement wall. He had barreled down the quiet road at 50 miles per hour. He had deliberately caused the horrible accident.[10]

- A Cincinnati, Ohio, teen went to a Christmas party with a friend. Friends at the party hoped the talented fifteen-year-old would play the piano and sing. Instead, she began inhaling the butane that she had earlier tucked into her pocket. The teen with the "voice of an angel" passed out and died a few hours later.[11]

four

Dangers of Inhalants

Since ancient times, people have inhaled substances to get intoxicated, or high. The ancient Greeks inhaled carbon dioxide to get high. The ancient Egyptians used skin creams and perfumes for religious ceremonies. Other ancient peoples inhaled burnt spices, gums, herbs, and incense during religious ceremonies.

History

In 1772, Sir Joseph Priestley was the first to prepare nitrous oxide. It was first used in 1844 by a Hartford, Connecticut, dentist. People called it laughing gas because it made them feel happy. Nitrous oxide parties became fashionable with people who did not know its dangers. While at one of these parties, Humphrey Davy, a famous doctor, saw that this gas killed pain. He began to

Sir Joseph Priestley (left) was the first to prepare nitrous oxide in 1772. Doctor Humphrey Davy (right), began to use nitrous oxide as an anesthetic in 1798.

use it as an anesthetic. Anesthetics are chemicals that stop people from feeling pain during surgery. Other new gases soon joined nitrous oxide, including chloroform and ether.

By the early 1900s, new products were created from petroleum. These products included solvents, thinners, and glues. Petroleum is a thick, oily, yellowish-black liquid mixture. It occurs naturally, usually below ground.

Some people inhaled these new products to get high. The first big inhalant craze hit in the late 1950s—sniffing glue and metallic paints. By the 1960s, this craze had slowed down. Many people thought inhalant abuse had disappeared.

Unfortunately, inhalant use resurfaced in the late 1980s. That is when national surveys began to show an increase in inhalant use. Since then, inhalant use has continued to increase every year, especially among younger teens.

Inhalants Defined

Inhalants are a large group of common products used in the house, school, garage, or workshop. They are either gases or liquids that vaporize (form gases) at room temperature. About fourteen hundred ordinary products can be inhaled. Users of these products huff, inhale through the mouth, or sniff, inhale through the nose.

People can walk into a grocery, hardware, or convenience store and buy these chemicals. Some look no further than their school or home. A typical house averages between thirty and sixty inhalant products.

Experts group inhalants into four types: solvents, aerosols, gases, and nitrates. Solvents are usually liquid substances. They can dissolve other things. Aerosols are substances that are released from a pressurized container. Gases include any substance that has no shape or volume but can expand indefinitely. Nitrates are saltlike compounds that can be inhaled.

In Then Out

When someone sniffs or huffs inhalants, the toxic fumes (poisonous gases) go right into the lungs, then into the bloodstream. The blood speeds the toxic chemicals to the muscles and major organs: liver, kidneys, heart, and brain. The brain controls all parts of the body.

Inhalants are exhaled by the lungs and through the

Types of Inhalants

Type of Inhalant	Examples	
Solvents	Asthma sprays*	Household
	Correction fluid	glue/cememt
	Fingernail polish	Lighter fluid
	and remover	Paint/paint thinner
	Gasoline/kerosene	Paint remover
Aerosols	Deodorant spray	Hair spray
	Fabric protector	Spray paint
	spray	
Gases	Butane	Propane
	Helium	Whippets
	Nitrous oxide	
Nitrates	Room deodorizers	
	Butyl (video head cleaner)	

*Asthma sprays are prescription medicines. A doctor must write a prescription, or instructions, so that someone with asthma can buy these sprays. Asthma, a chronic disease, causes chest tightness, coughing, and breathing problems. When used properly, asthma sprays help people with asthma breathe easier. No one should ever use any medication prescribed for another person.

kidneys and skin. The inhalant odor can be smelled on an abuser's breath or through the skin. The body can take two or more weeks to get rid of these toxic chemicals. But not all of the toxic chemicals are ever removed. Some are stored in the body's fat, including the fatty tissue in the brain, kidneys, liver, heart, and muscles. The brain is made up of one-third fatty tissues.

Mark Groves, director of the Minnesota Eden Children's Project, often speaks to students around the state about inhalant abuse. He explains that inhalants are poisonous chemicals. "They were never meant for human consumption [use], and are more closely related to pesticides than they are to marijuana or cocaine."[1] Pesticides are toxic chemicals used to kill harmful animals or plants, especially insects and rodents.

To help young people better understand the dangers of inhalants, Groves talks about a 1992 chemical spill

 The Big Three

Solvents are the most often abused inhalants. The three most commonly abused solvents are toluene, trichloroethylene, and gasoline. Here are some facts about them.

Solvent	Inhalants That Contain the Solvent	Toxic Effects of Ongoing Use
Toluene	Cleaning agents Glues Inks Paints Thinners	Causes trembling. Affects balance, hearing, vision, reasoning. Damages the nervous system.
Trichloroethylene	Correction fluids Paints Spot removers	Drunkenlike behavior. Can cause hallucinations. Affects balance, hearing, vision, reasoning. Damages the nervous system.
Gasoline	Gasoline contains toxic metals, solvents, and other chemicals.	Sleeping problems, trembling, extreme weight loss, paralysis. If leaded gas is used: hallucinations, convulsions.

between Superior, Wisconsin, and Duluth, Minnesota. A train carrying benzene, a toxic chemical, derailed between the two cities. The benzene spilled out of the tanker cars and into the Nemadji River. The fumes from the benzene created a cloud in the air. All freeways, highways, and streets going into and out of both cities were blocked. Over sixty thousand people had to leave their homes so they would not inhale the benzene. This ranked as the largest forced exit of people in the history of the United States.[2]

Benzene Danger!

Why the Concern?	Because of the Danger Level
Health professionals and city officials were concerned about the people in the area.	The danger level of benzene was at five parts per million (PPM) in eight hours.
Kids who huff or sniff inhalants should be concerned.	They inhale the same or similar chemicals at ten thousand to thirty thousands parts per million within a few seconds.

Initial Effects

Because inhalants speed their way to the brain, the high they produce comes very quickly, within seven to ten seconds. Inhalant highs generally run from a few minutes to sixty minutes. At first, users may feel somewhat stimulated, light-headed, numb, or excited.

Soon, though, inhalants start working on the central nervous system (CNS). The CNS includes the brain and spinal cord. Inhalants depress or slow down the CNS. As a result, users may feel less inhibited or restrained, less in control, light-headed and giddy. They may act drunk, feel dizzy and sleepy, slur their speech, and walk unsteadily. Because judgment is impaired or weakened, users sometimes make unsafe or risky decisions. This increases their chance of being in or causing an accident and injury.

If users take in large amounts of inhalants, the CNS is hit harder. Hallucinations, or imaginary sights, sounds, and smells, may occur. Users may become dazed and dreamy, and fall asleep. Or they may go into a coma or die.

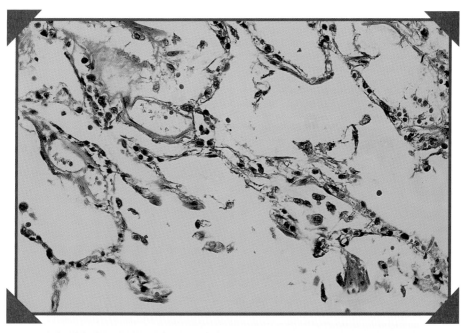

Healthy lung tissue is shown here. When someone sniffs or huffs inhalants, the toxic (poisonous) fumes go right into the lungs—causing severe damage, even death.

Headaches, nausea, and feeling down often follow the high. These effects can last for days.

Continued Use

If inhalant use continues, more effects can occur: headaches, nausea or vomiting, mood changes, hallucinations, dizziness, loss of concentration, confusion, and loss of balance are common. Poor judgment and violent or aggressive behavior sometimes occur.

Inhalant abusers can never be sure of exactly what chemicals they inhale. Most inhalants contain many different ingredients. Some are highly toxic. Most solvents and aerosols contain toxic additives. Depending on the chemicals inhaled or sniffed, users can cause serious damage to their bodies. Sometimes this damage is permanent and cannot be reversed. Hardest hit are the brain, nervous system, liver, kidneys, blood, and bone marrow.

Some users go blind, have memory problems, or have permanent brain damage. Learning disabilities can result. The toxic chemical benzene, found in rubber cement, can cause cancer. Hearing loss can occur from abusing paint sprays, glues, dewaxers, cleaning fluids, and correction fluids. Sniffing lead-based gasoline or paint can lead to lead poisoning.

Focus on the Brain

Friends and family noticed that Joe had changed. Once athletic, friendly, and a good student, the teen had become violent and irregular in his behavior. Concerned, Joe's mother took him to a doctor. The doctor found that Joe had already damaged his brain from abusing spray paint. But Joe continued huffing over the next few years. Finally, he was sent to the Colorado Mental Health Institute in Pueblo.

Joe once spoke English and Spanish with ease. Now in his early thirties, Joe has lost most of his memory. Nothing can replace the brain cells destroyed by inhalants. He cannot form sentences that make sense.

Dr. Milton Tenebein treats children and teen inhalant abusers at the Children's Hospital in Winnipeg, Canada. Over the years, he has seen many teens like Joe with brain damage from using inhalants. He has also found teens who damaged their lungs and kidneys and became deaf from inhalants. Sometimes a child or teen becomes paralyzed after just six months of heavy abuse. According to Dr. Tenebein, people who abuse inhalants long enough will eventually damage their brain. This damage cannot be repaired.

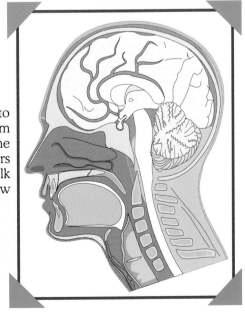

Inhalants work their way into the central nervous system (CNS). The CNS includes the brain and spinal cord. Users may feel dizzy, sleepy, or walk unsteadily, as inhalants slow down the CNS.

Inhalant Usage

Using inhalants just once, you could

- feel your hands and feet tingle and go numb;
- have severe mood swings;
- have hallucinations—imaginary sights, sounds, or smells;
- have trouble breathing; or
- die suddenly.

Using inhalants for a short period, you could

- feel dizzy;
- get headaches;
- have rapid heartbeats;
- have trouble breathing; or
- die suddenly.

Using inhalants over a longer period, you could

- be thirsty constantly;
- become violent and hurt yourself or other people;
- damage brain, liver, lungs, kidneys, and nervous system;
- damage memory, vision, hearing;
- develop a constant cough;
- develop hepatitis (painful inflammation of the liver);
- feel nauseated, dizzy, numb, or tired;
- experience excessive weight loss;
- get headaches, muscle weakness, and stomach pains;
- have no control over passing urine or bowel movements;
- have rashes around the nose or mouth; or
- die suddenly.

Researchers know that if users continue to abuse inhalants, brain damage will occur. That is because inhalants reduce the supply of oxygen to the brain. Brain cells die without enough oxygen. Once brain cells die, they are never replaced. So brain damage from inhalants is permanent.

Over time, repeat inhalant users will have poor memories and slow, irregular responses. They cannot do simple math easily. Other problems such as shaking or trembling, poor coordination, and trouble with walking can result.

Focus on the Lungs

Breathing is automatic, something the body does on its own, twelve to eighteen times a minute. You usually do not think about how you get oxygen from the air around you. Thanks to the lungs and heart, oxygen is taken in and moves to the body's cells and organs. The lungs take in air and pass oxygen from the air to the blood. Then the fist-sized heart pumps oxygen-rich blood through the body. Blood can travel from the heart to the big toe and back in less than one minute.

In addition to inhaling oxygen and breathing out carbon dioxide, a waste gas, the lungs perform other tasks. They add moisture to the air breathed in and bring the air to proper body temperature. The lungs also clean out unwanted substances. When people use inhalants, their lungs become damaged and cannot carry out their tasks as well.

People who sniff inhalants can damage their lungs, throat, mouth, and nose. This damage shows up when users complain of a sore throat or nose, sores around the nose or mouth, sneezing, coughing, or chest pain.

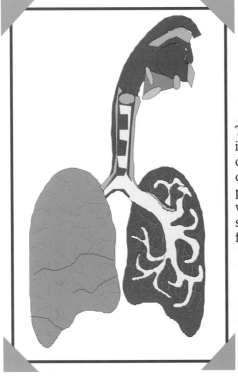

The lungs perform the important job of inhaling oxygen and breathing out carbon dioxide waste. When people damage their lungs with inhalants, the lungs struggle to perform these functions.

Inhalant abuse also can make the lining of the nose, mouth, throat, and lungs break down. This allows infections such as pneumonia and bronchitis to develop more easily.

Sniffing spray inhalants is especially dangerous. Spray inhalants coat the lungs with a gooey film. Then not enough oxygen can get through the lungs into the bloodstream. Sometimes this results in death.

The Risk of SSD

Another serious problem, sudden sniffing death (SSD), can happen with inhalant abuse. When users inhale concentrated chemical fumes, they can die of cardiac arrest (heart attack) or suffocation.

Common Inhalants and Their Effects

Inhaled Substance	What It Does to the Body Over Time
Plastic Cements	Brain and nervous system damage from chronic use. Possible liver and kidney damage.
Modeling glues or cements	Brain and kidney damage from chronic use. Possible liver damage.
Rubber cement	Liver, kidney, and bone marrow damage. Anemia (condition of low red blood cell count), leukemia (a cancer), and damage to cells.
Fingernail polish remover	Kidney damage. Possible liver damage.
Lacquer thinner	Brain damage from chronic use. Possible liver and kidney damage.
Cleaning fluids (spot removers and shoe cleaner)	Possible liver and kidney damage. Nausea, vomiting, weight loss.
Gasoline	Brain damage. Lead poisoning from sniffing leaded gasoline.
Aerosols	Irregular heartbeat and heart failure can result. Lungs stop working and person can die.

Freddy, a lively sixteen-year-old, was a computer whiz. One hot August morning, Freddy's dad called for his son to wake up. Thinking that his son had overslept, Freddy's father opened the bedroom door. Freddy was lying across his bed. His father shook Freddy, but he would not wake up. As his father turned away, he saw a can of air freshener beside his son. Freddy had died from SSD.

The chemicals in solvents and aerosol sprays can make the heart beat fast and erratically. This dangerous condition is called arrhythmia, meaning irregular rhythm. The overworked heart may suddenly stop beating or pumping blood, and the person dies. That is cardiac arrest. The director of the Minnesota Eden Children's Project, Mark Groves, explains another risk of inhalants. "Inhale them and the heartbeat can change from a calm 70 to 110 beats per minute to an erratic 150 to 200 beats per minute."[3] Such a fast heartbeat can end in a heart attack. Or the inhalant can starve the body of oxygen by pushing air out of the lungs. Breathing stops and the person dies instantly.

No one can predict the amount needed for an inhalant to kill. A teen can sniff or huff a certain amount one time and live. But the next time, that same amount can kill. Or a teen can inhale once—and die.

Inhalant's Hook

Over time, with repeated sniffing or huffing, users can develop a tolerance. Tolerance means that a person's body requires more and more of the drug to get the same initial effects. These larger and larger amounts of inhalants multiply the many risks connected with inhalant abuse. According to medical experts, death from inhalants can occur in five ways.

Common Forms of Inhalant-Related Deaths

- Asphyxia—the toxic gases from inhalants can limit oxygen in the air going into the lungs. Breathing then stops.

- Careless behaviors in risky situations

- Choking on vomit

- Sudden death from the heart stopping (SSD)

- Suffocation—lack of oxygen to the lungs, typically seen with inhalant users who use bags.

Some inhalant abusers become preoccupied with the feelings they get from inhalants. When this happens, they can no longer control their use of inhalants and have become dependent on them. Dependence is a special problem for teens. The constant need for and abuse of inhalants can interfere with a teen's physical, mental, and emotional development.

When users who are dependent on inhalants stop using them, they go through withdrawal. Withdrawal is the process of ridding the body of a drug. Withdrawal can produce many symptoms: anxiety, feeling down, headaches, stomach pains, nausea, muscle cramps, shaking, sweating, hostility, and hallucinations. Some will continue to crave inhalants. Withdrawal symptoms can last for several days.

At age fifteen, Elizabeth and her friends began sniffing Scotchgard™ or nitrous oxide before going to the movies. At first, Elizabeth's use was occasional and only with her friends. But within six months, the Denver teen only wanted to sniff inhalants. She no longer did anything with her friends. She remembers, "I didn't care about the headaches and that it made me throw up. The high was all that mattered."[4]

By the time she became a senior, Elizabeth had lost a lot of weight. Every morning the mirror reflected back ugly rashes around her nose and mouth. "I was distraught over what I'd done with my life. I had been a genuinely happy person before, and now I was happy only when I had this drug."[5] On her own, Elizabeth quit. Since then, she has successfully stayed off of inhalants.

Fetal Solvent Syndrome

If a woman is pregnant, inhaling chemicals can damage her developing baby. Sometimes inhalants end the pregnancy. Sometimes they damage the growing baby. At birth, these babies may have a small head, deep-set eyes, disfigured nose and ears, stubby fingers, and damaged nerves and kidneys. The baby's growth may be slow, and the baby's attention span may be short. These problems resulting from inhalant use during pregnancy are known as fetal solvent syndrome.

five

Fighting Inhalant Abuse

Two keys to combating inhalant abuse are awareness and education. State programs, schools, communities, and individuals can provide information, education, and help in dealing with inhalant abuse.

Schools provide a great way to teach about the dangers of inhalants. One example of someone who works through the schools is Marla Stewart, a school nurse for Kirby Public Schools. She talks about inhalant abuse to fifth to ninth graders. At each presentation, a guest speaker discusses her cousin who sniffed butane at the age of sixteen. He now lives in a nursing home, with the mental abilities of a baby.[1]

State Efforts to Combat Abuse

Many states are battling inhalant abuse in various ways. Here are what three states are doing.

The Illinois' Campaign. The lieutenant governor's office in Illinois began a statewide campaign on inhalant abuse in 1994. This ongoing campaign is called "Danger: Right Under Your Nose." It provides materials, tools, and ideas that communities and people can use to get the message out about inhalants. There is also a toll-free phone number people can call for more information.

The Minnesota Eden Children's Project. Since 1990, the Eden Children's Project has been developing and running inhalant prevention programs. The state of Minnesota contracts with this project to provide the following:

- education and training about inhalant abuse prevention and treatment; and

- services to preteens and teens abusing inhalants and other drugs and to their families.

Currently, the Eden Children's Project has offices in the Minneapolis-St. Paul area and a rural location. Each year, it provides services to more than one hundred families with teen and preteen inhalant users. It also averages more than two hundred education and training seminars. In addition, this group partners with other Minnesota state and retail groups to increase awareness of inhalant abuse. The Eden Children's Project has developed inhalant abuse materials for students.

The director of the Eden Children's Project, Mark Groves, often speaks to students around the state. Then he shows a videotape. In the video, a teen named Lenny sits on a hospital bed. He is shaking from head to toe. When the doctor asks Lenny to walk, he can barely walk the length of the bed. The doctor has to help him. Lenny started sniffing when he was nine. He was seventeen when the video was made. Inhalants had destroyed or badly damaged part of his brain.[2] Groves usually ends by telling kids to make the wise decision about inhalant and drug use—not to give in to peer pressure.

The New Jersey Governor's Council on Alcohol and Drug Abuse. The New Jersey Governor's Council on Alcohol and Drug Abuse has taken inhalant abuse awareness and prevention statewide. Each year, twenty-one counties participate in National Inhalant Prevention and Awareness Week (NIPAW). John Kriger, chief of training, offers workshops to educate PTAs, police officers, and other groups about inhalant abuse. Kriger's program called "What's Hot, What's Not" shows adults what to look for and how to handle inhalant abuse.

Communities

Various communities, some local and others national, are working to combat inhalant abuse. Here are some examples of what they are doing.

PTA. Since 1994 the Parent Teacher Association (PTA) has worked to increase public awareness about inhalants. This education and parent organization has millions of members worldwide. The PTA encourages its members to hold inhalant abuse awareness workshops or meetings. One example is the Maple Crest Elementary and Middle School PTA in Kokomo, Indiana. This PTA held an evening workshop to educate parents about inhalant abuse. Nursing students from the local university and a police officer presented a program and passed out information.

National Inhalant Prevention Coalition. The Texas Presentation Partnership founded the National Inhalant Prevention Coalition in 1993. Director Harvey Weiss has appeared on many television and radio talk shows and in hundreds of magazine, newspaper, and newsletter articles. This Austin organization

- provides resources to support inhalant prevention and treatment;

- promotes a national campaign that explains the dangers of inhalants; and

- holds an Inhalants and Poisons Awareness Week during the third week in March each year. More than one thousand organizations from nearly all the states participate in this event. This campaign has become a model in the fight against inhalant abuse.

Partnership for a Drug-Free America. The Partnership for a Drug-Free America began a campaign in 1995 to tell the public about the dangers of inhalant abuse. This

Teens need to be made aware of the fact that inhalants, although they may come in the form of common household products, are actually deadly toxic (poisonous) chemicals.

campaign distributes print and television warning ads to America's forty largest media markets. The Partnership for a Drug-Free America is a volunteer organization of communications companies.

Poison Control Centers. Poison Control Centers across the United States provide information on the problem of inhalant abuse. They can help evaluate the chemicals in inhalants and the best treatment. Poison Control Centers are involved in informational and awareness prevention campaigns and programs that teach kids about chemical safety.

International Institute for Inhalant Abuse. The International Institute for Inhalant Abuse (IIIA) is based in Englewood, Colorado. Led by medical director Dr. Neil Rosenberg, the IIIA

- ◆ researches inhalant abuse and the effect on the body and mind;

- ◆ educates children, teens, parents, educators, criminal justice professionals, and health care professionals about inhalants through workshops, seminars, presentations, and seminars; and

- ◆ develops and shares materials such as brochures, posters, educational kits, articles, and stickers to increase awareness of inhalant abuse.

The Elks. The Elks society is located in nearly twenty-three hundred communities nationwide and counts more than one million members. The Elks National Drug Awareness Program "honors and educates young people who are willing to be part of the solution rather than part of the problem," says Andy Milwid, executive director.[3] The Elks drug prevention program provides material for fourth through ninth grade students on various drugs, including inhalants. Students receive drug prevention brochures, coloring materials, and participate in poster contests aimed at prevention. More than 3 million kids in the United States have been part of the Elks "Hoop Shoot" Free Throw Contest. This contest is held each year.

Individuals

Just one person can make a big difference in the fight against inhalant abuse. Here are two mothers who have taken on the challenge of informing kids and adults about the dangers of inhalants.

Grace Jones

In a middle school in her hometown of Palm Beach Gardens, Florida, Grace Jones holds up a photo of Jennifer. The six hundred students quiet down as the small woman speaks about her daughter Jennifer. "She was the outgoing one. I've always hated speaking in front of a crowd. But she can't be here. She died from huffing inhalants."[4]

Jones tells the hushed assembly what happened. On June 5, 1994, she called Jennifer, nicknamed J.J., inside for dinner. There was no response. Hours passed, but J.J. never appeared. Neither she nor her husband, Richard, could find her. Later the sheriff found J.J. right by the house, under the air-conditioning unit. The lively teen had died from inhaling Freon, a gas used in air conditioners.

The Joneses had never heard of huffing inhalants. They knew their daughter opposed illegal drugs. "She told other kids that drugs would mess up their lives and that they shouldn't do them," Jones remembered.[5] But a boy at school convinced J.J. to try huffing. He told J.J. it was not like taking drugs.

Just three days after her daughter's death, Grace Jones appeared on the local news to talk about huffing. The next day she repeated her information to a Miami station. She now works to get newspapers to run articles about huffing and to provide help to people across the United States. She has talked at many school programs and on television talk shows. Her information has appeared in national and local magazines and newspapers. Armed with hundreds of petitions from around the country, Jones has asked that the federal government raise national awareness about inhalant abuse. She wants the president to create a national inhalant awareness week. The memory of her daughter drives Jones. "By doing this work, I keep J.J.'s spirit alive."[6]

Getting the message out about the dangers of inhalants is important. If more parents who have lost teens to inhalant abuse spoke out, perhaps that message would sink in.

Susan Wilson-Tucker

"My daughter Jennifer hated drugs. She thought using them was stupid," said Susan Wilson-Tucker of Hampton, Georgia.[7] In October 1994, Jennifer, age fifteen, and her boyfriend, Jason, were passengers in a car driven by a third teen, Bradley. Bradley, age seventeen, was sniffing computer cleaning fluid to get high. He passed out and hit a truck. Jennifer died instantly and her boyfriend was badly injured. Bradley got a few scratches. Neither Jennifer nor Jason had huffed any inhalants, taken drugs, or drunk alcohol.

Susan Wilson-Tucker, a nurse, decided to help others with information about inhalants. First, she read everything she could find. Then, she contacted schools to give presentations. After her presentations on inhalants, kids would come up to her and tell her their stories. One eleven-year-old told her that he often huffed gasoline but did not know that it was dangerous. Other teens told her that students sniffed inhalants in classes and sometimes passed out. In addition to her presentations, Susan Wilson-Tucker has

- ◆ successfully worked to get the state of Georgia to include inhalants in the Driving Under the Influence (DUI) law;

- ◆ helped develop inhalant education materials for schools; and

- ◆ been on numerous national and local television talk shows and appeared in magazine and newspaper articles.

Jennifer's older brother, Casey, has enrolled in the police academy. After he graduates, he plans to do his part to stop people who drive under the influence of drugs.

six

What You Can Do

Peer pressure is a big reason that teens give when asked why they use inhalants and other drugs. Everyone wants to be liked and accepted by others. But each person can and should decide for himself or herself what to put in the body.

Saying No to Inhalants

It is not always easy to say no. Saying no to inhalants and other drugs takes courage. However, refusing to use inhalants or take drugs shows respect for yourself and for your body. It says that you are responsible for what you do, and decide not to do.

Quitting

If you or someone you know wants to quit using inhalants or other drugs, talk to any of the following:

49

- family or friends;

- teachers, school counselors, drug abuse counselors, your doctor, or other health professionals;

- hot lines and referral services;

- drug treatment programs or chemical dependency programs;

- mental health agencies;

- organizations in your area. Look in the telephone book's yellow pages under "Drug Abuse."

 Three Steps to Saying No to Drugs

If someone wants you to do something and you are not sure what to decide, follow these three steps:

1. Figure out whether what your friend wants you to do is OK. To do this, ask yourself, "Is this safe?" or "Will this get me into trouble?" or "Would my parents approve?" or "Would I feel right doing this?"

2. If your answer is no, say "No" or "No thanks" to your friend. When you say no, sound firm and confident. You can also shake your head no, fold your arms across your chest, or put your hands in your pockets. These actions and your refusal tell the other person that you mean no.

3. Now suggest other things to do that are fun and safe. Be upbeat and positive about your ideas.

If the other person keeps trying to convince you to say yes, walk away.

Tell Others About Inhalant Abuse

To help get information out about the dangers of inhalant abuse, here are some steps you can take:

- Create posters that warn about inhalant abuse. Include telephone numbers of places people can call for help or for more information. Ask the owners or managers of places that kids and teens often go to if you can put up your posters. Try recreation centers, record stores, fast-food restaurants, pizza places, ice-cream parlors, candy stores, movie theaters, supermarkets, and youth centers.

- Write a letter about inhalant abuse to the editor of your community and local newspapers.

- Use facts to create your own brochures about inhalant abuse. Include telephone numbers of places that people can call for help or for more information. Ask local supermarkets whether they will stuff your fact sheet in customers' bags.

- Ask local businesses, such as the gas or telephone company, to include bill stuffers about the dangers of inhalant abuse.

Enjoy Drug-Free Fun

Looking good and feeling good are great reasons to avoid using inhalants and other drugs. Millions of kids and teens across the United States stay free of inhalants and other harmful substances. They know that using drugs does not solve problems or add anything rewarding to their lives.

There are lots of ways to enjoy life. For example, learn a new skill. Learning to play a musical instrument can be fun. So can learning a new language, taking dance lessons, or trying out for a play. Skating, rollerblading, water or snow skiing, or skateboarding are other options. There are also plenty of sports to try—tennis, volleyball, soccer, basketball, baseball, hockey, or track, are just a few.

Creative writing or art are other fun activities. Many magazines publish young people's stories or poems.

Volunteers who work at a hospital, day care center, food bank, nature center, or nursing home are always in demand. Volunteers also teach people to read or read for people who have trouble seeing.

Baby-sitting, doing yard work, cleaning basements or

Regular exercise is a healthy, fun activity that keeps the body and mind active.

attics, washing cars, or doing other odd jobs can be profitable and fun.

Peer support groups at schools can help kids discuss and deal with daily life issues and decisions, offer fun activities, and sometimes increase cultural awareness. After school youth programs or groups such as Boys and Girls Clubs of America, Cub Scouts, Boy Scouts, and Girl Scouts offer many activities. Belonging to groups like these is a great way to meet new friends and do exciting activities and projects.

Peer leadership programs and peer counseling interventions exist at many schools or community centers. These programs help kids learn how to speak before an audience, organize tasks, talk with peers and adults, and run group meetings. Peer leaders sometimes speak at conferences and meetings or colead drug prevention activities. Peer counseling interventions involve kids who help their peers through one-on-one sessions, informal street talks, or answering a telephone hot line.

Here are some examples of what kids are doing as peer leaders and peer counselors.

- Each year in Kyle, South Dakota, selected students at Little Wound School are trained as peer counselors. They learn how to counsel groups and individuals. Peer counselors give presentations on drug abuse in their communities and school. They also carry out other projects to lessen drug use.

- Young people in Atlanta, Georgia, can join a program called Super Stars. Super Stars sessions are held in the early evening at a school or community center. There young people learn about drug abuse and how to say no to drugs. They

Peer counselors, young people who help other young people deal with their problems, are an important resource in the battle against inhalant abuse.

also develop decision-making skills and build their confidence with fun activities.

♦ Everyday Theater serves African-American preteens and teens in Washington, D.C. Each year, the program includes a summer theater for kids, an on-the-job training program for older teens, and an after-school program for all. Kids in Everyday Theater help develop an original play. They then perform the play in eighteen places throughout Washington, D.C. In this way, Everyday Theater reaches thousands of preteens and teens with information about drug abuse.

♦ Project Venture in New Mexico, which is held every

year in four American Indian communities, includes summer leadership camps and year-round programs and activities in schools and communities. Project Venture gives kids the chance to enjoy drug-free fun such as camping trips, rock climbing, rappelling, rope courses, and canoeing. In addition, older teens are trained to become big brothers and big sisters to younger kids. This project has the only fully certified search and rescue teams in the United States made up of all American Indian students.

questions for discussion

1. Before reading this book, did you know what inhalants were? Did you think of inhalants as drugs that can be abused?

2. How many kids do you know who have used or are using inhalants? How do you feel about their inhalant use?

3. What are some ways of refusing drugs that you would feel comfortable using?

4. Has anyone tried to get you to use inhalants? If yes, how did you handle it? What do you wish you had done differently?

5. Are inhalants talked about in your school's drug education classes? If not, would you recommend that inhalants be included?

6. If you have younger brothers or sisters, will you tell them about inhalant abuse? If they are five years old or younger, would you put poison stickers on cans and bottles of inhalants in your house?

7. Suppose a friend is using an inhalant, but suddenly falls down, unconscious. What would you do?

8. Make a list of all the inhalants in your home. How many different ones did you find? Are you surprised at how many you found?

9. Look at five spray cans in your home. Do they have warning labels? If yes, do you think they are effective?

chapter notes

Chapter 1. Ian's Story

All notes in this chapter taken from: "Ian's Story: If I Knew What Inhalants Can Do, I Would Never Have Started," May 16, 1997, (Minneapolis, Minn.: The Eden Children's Project), unpaged.

Chapter 2. The Silent Epidemic

1. *Inhalants: The Silent Epidemic* (Austin, Tex.: National Inhalant Prevention Coalition, 1997), p. 5.

2. Ibid., p. 9.

3. Romel Hernandez, "Englewood Girl, 11, 'Critical' After Sniffing Hair Spray," *Rocky Mountain News*, June 7, 1993, p. IIIA.

4. *What Communities Can Do About Inhalant Abuse*, (Englewood, Colo.: International Institute on Inhalant Abuse, 1996).

5. "Ian's Story: If I Knew What Inhalants Can Do, I Would Never Have Started," May 16, 1997 (Minneapolis, Minn.: The Eden Children's Project), unpaged.

6. *What Communities Can Do About Inhalant Abuse.*

7. National Inhalant Prevention Coalition, "Surveys Show Inhalants Continue to Rise," *ViewPoint*, Fall/Winter 1996, p. 3.

8. Ibid., p. 5.

9. *Tips for Teens About Inhalants* (Substance Abuse and Mental Health Services Administration, 1997), unpaged.

10. *What Communities Can Do About Inhalant Abuse.*

11. *Inhalants: The Silent Epidemic*, p. 9.

12. "Ian's Story."

13. *Inhalant Abuse Prevention Seminar* (Minneapolis, Minn.: The Eden Children's Project, 1996), p. 5.

14. Myra Weatherly, *Inhalants* (Springfield, N.J.: Enslow Publishers, Inc. 1996), p. 58.

15. Ibid.

16. Darryl S., Inaba, William E. Cohen, and Michael E. Holstein, *Uppers, Downers, All Arounders: Physical and Mental Effects of Psychoactive Drugs* (Ashland, Oreg.: CNS Publications, Inc., 1997), p. 258.

17. "State X State Inhalant Legislation," *ViewPoint*, Spring 1997, p. 5.

18. Bob Trebilcock, "The New High Kids Crave: One Family's Tragedy," *Redbook*, March 1993, p. 76.

19. Ibid., pp. 76–77.

20, Ibid., p. 78.

21. Ibid., p. 118.

22. Ibid.

Chapter 3. Real-Life Stories

1. Juan Espinosa, "Sniffing Paint Nearly Ruined the Lives of Liz, Billie," *Chieftain & Star Journal*, April 18, 1993, pp. 1B, 3B.

2. Ibid.

3. Daryl S. Inaba, William E. Cohen, and Michael E. Holstein, *Uppers, Downers, All Arounders: Physical and Mental Effects of Psychoactive Drugs* (Ashland, Oreg.: CNS Productions, Inc., 1997), p. 262.

4. International Institute on Inhalant Abuse, "Deaths Related to Inhalant Abuse," undated pamphlet.

5. Inaba, et al., p. 258.

6. International Institute on Inhalant Abuse.

7. Anita Bartholomew, "Is Your Child Huffing?" *Readers Digest*, May 1996, p. 131.

8. International Institute on Inhalant Abuse.

9. Ibid.

10. Tim McLaughlin, "Chief: Crash Was Intentional," *St. Joseph News*, February 11, 1994, pp. 1A–2A.

11. B.G. Gregg, "Mom: Daughter, 15, Alone to Blame for Fatal Overdose," *The Cincinnati Enquirer*, December 27, 1994, pp. C1, C5.

Chapter 4. Dangers of Inhalants

1. Rick Olivo, "Inhalant Abuse: The Kids 'Cheap' High," *The Daily Press*, October 7, 1993, p. 1.

2. Lee Sevig, "The Sniff That Snuffs Out Life," *Advocate Tribune*, November 18, 1993, p. 1A.

3. Ibid.

4. "Fatal Attraction: How 'Huffing' Kills," *Redbook*, March, 1993, p. 120.

5. Ibid.

Chapter 5. Fighting Inhalant Abuse

1. Marla Stewart, "Letter to the Editor," *ViewPoint*, Summer 1997, p. 13.

2. Lee Sevig, "The Sniff That Snuffs Out Life," *Advocate Tribune*, November 18, 1993, p. 1A.

3. "Elks Prevention Efforts Span Nation," *ViewPoint*, Spring 1997, p. 10.

4. Anita Bartholomew, "Keeping a Child's Spirit Alive," *Good Housekeeping*, May 1996, p. 28.

5. Ibid.

6. Ibid.

7. Susan Wilson-Tucker and Judi Dash, "Legal but Lethal," *Family Circle*, October 10, 1995, p. 21.

Chapter 6. What You Can Do

No notes.

where to go for help

Indiana Prevention Resource Center
<http://www.drugs.indiana.edu>

Join Together Online
<http://www.jointogether.org>

National Families in Action
2957 Clairmont Road
Suite 150
Atlanta, GA 30329
(404) 248-9676
<http://www.emory.edu/NFIA/>

National Inhalant Prevention Coalition
1201 W. Sixth Street
Suite C-200
Austin, TX 78703
(800) 269-4237
<http://www.inhalants.org>

NIDA Info Fax
1-888-644-6432
<http://www.nida.nih.gov>

Our Home, Inc.
360 Ohio SW
Huron, SD 57350
(605) 352-4368

Inhalant treatment program for teens

Wisconsin Clearinghouse, University of Wisconsin-Madison University Health Services
<http://www.uhs.wisc.edu/wch>

acquired immunodeficiency syndrome (AIDS)—A deadly disorder of the immune system. It lowers the body's ability to fight off infectious bacteria and viruses.

addict—A person who is dependent on a drug.

aerosol—A mixture of gas and tiny particles of a liquid or solid.

arrhythmia—An irregular heartbeat rhythm.

benzene—A clear, colorless liquid that burns easily. It is derived from petroleum and is used to make detergents, insect poisons, motor fuels, and other chemicals.

butane—A gas obtained from petroleum used as a fuel and to make synthetic rubber.

carcinogen—A substance that tends to cause cancer.

epidemic—A fast-growing problem across a large area.

ether—An organic compound used to produce anesthesia.

fetal solvent syndrome (FSS)—Physical or mental defects to the child of a mother who abused solvents during her pregnancy.

Freon™—One of a class of chemicals that contributes to destroying the ozone layer. Used in aerosols.

fumes—Gases.

hallucination—Imaginary sights, sounds, tastes, and smells.

huffing—Soaking a rag with inhalant, putting the rag over the mouth and nose, and inhaling. Also the slang term for any kind of inhaling.

human immunodeficiency virus (HIV)—The virus that causes AIDS.

inhalants—A large group of common products that are either gases or liquids that vaporize or form gases at room temperature.

nitrous oxide—A gas used in dentistry as an anesthetic and in aerosol cans.

pesticides—Toxic chemicals used to kill harmful animals or plants, especially insects and rodents.

petroleum—A thick, oily, yellowish-black liquid mixture. It occurs naturally, usually below ground.

poppers—Street name for amyl nitrite.

sniffing—Breathing in an inhalant directly from the container.

solvent—A liquid substance that can dissolve one or more other substances.

sudden sniffing death (SSD)—Sudden death as a result of inhalation of chemical substances. It can happen with first-time use or regular use.

tolerance—A person's body requiring more and more of a drug to get the same initial effects.

toluene—A liquid solvent used in many industrial products such as glues, paints, and thinners. Toluene is often abused as an inhalant.

toxin—Poisonous chemicals.

vaporize—Substances that form gases at room temperature.

withdrawal—The process of ridding the body of a drug.

further reading

The Challenge: Focus on Inhalants. Washington, D.C.: U.S. Department of Education, vol. 5, no. 4.

Clifford, Sherry. *Inhalants*. New York: Rosen Publishing Group, 1994.

Dubois, Ann. *Inhalant Update*. Atlanta, Ga.: National Families in Action, 1997.

Glowa, John R. *Inhalants*. New York: Chelsea House, 1992.

Inhalants & Their Effects. Northfield, Minn.: Life Skills Education, 1992.

Monroe, Judy. "Inhalants: Dangerous Highs," *Current Health 2*. September 1995.

Substance Abuse and Mental Health Services Administration. *Tips for Teens: Inhalants*. Washington, D.C.: U.S. Department of Health and Human Services.

Weatherly, Myra. *Inhalants*. Springfield, N.J.: Enslow Publishers, Inc. 1996.

Internet Addresses

Alcohol, Tobacco, and Other Drugs Resource Guide
<http://www.health.org/pubs/resguide/inhalan.htm>

Inhalant Abuse
<http://www.jointogether.org/sa/issues/hot_issues/inhalants/>

index

DATE DUE

JAN 24			
JUN 2 200			
6			
DEC 1 0 2010			
JAN 3 200			
APR 2 4 2019			
DEC 1 8 2019			